First Love

Joyce Carol Oates

First Love

A GOTHIC TALE

Designed and Illustrated by Barry Moser

THE ECCO PRESS

Copyright © 1996 by The Ontario Review, Inc.
Illustrations copyright © 1996 by Barry Moser
All rights reserved
THE ECCO PRESS
100 West Broad Street
Hopewell, New Jersey 08525
Published simultaneously in Canada by Penguin Books
Canada Ltd., Ontario
Printed in the United States of America
Library of Congress Cataloging-in-Publication Data
Oates, Joyce Carol, 1938-
First love : a Gothic tale / Joyce Carol Oates ; illustrated by
Barry Moser.—1st ECCO ed.
p.   cm.
ISBN 0-88001-457-1 (alk. paper)
I. Title.
PS3565.A8F57   1996
813'.54—dc20   95-36354
CIP
Designed by Barry Moser, Hand lettering by Reassurance
Wunder
The text of this book is set in Eric Gill's Joanna.

9   8   7   6   5   4   3   2   1

FIRST EDITION

for Sharon Friedman

FIRST LOVE

THE BLACK SNAKE. Feel yourself drawn! Behind the tall house bearing shingles the color of pewter. Into the heat-shimmering marsh below, sloping to the Cassadaga River. Your first morning in Ransomville, you slip from your hard, unfamiliar bed, dress swiftly, and leave the house wanting to see the river close up. Sun on your forehead light as a warning slap, already it's hot before 8 A.M. Run, run! — feet sinking on the spongy earth. A fierce excited din of birds, bullfrogs, cicadas on all sides. At the bottom of the hill someone has laid planks down, into the marsh; you wonder if it's safe to walk on them, they're so rotted.

Fear is good, fear is normal. Fear will save your life.

Who has told you this, which adult, your mother, your father—or will it be Jared, Jr., to come?

Through a straggly stand of polelike barkless trees, you will learn are *bamboo*, the river shines bottle-green in the morning sun. Reflecting light like shattered glass. Which way is the river flowing, which way is north? North to Lake Oriskany? Hundreds of miles away.

On the farther shore of the river there's a gauzy mist. The backs of houses and buildings nearly obscured by trees, junglelike vegetation. You enter the marsh shyly, a strange sensation like floating walking on the planks; the marsh is living, the dark rich damp soil makes an oozing, bubbling sound. *The Cassadaga is a beautiful river,* your mother has said. *We'll be there, looking out onto it.*

From Mother you will inherit the belief that you can journey to your fate, there's a place to be located on a map that's destiny. If only you can get there. If only it isn't too late. If no one stops you.

Just inside the marsh, where some of the cattails, reeds, bamboo stalks tower over your head, you see it—something black moving swiftly and sinuously. Gleaming-glittering along its length, S-shaped, oily-black. A snake! Long as your arm! You have an impression of an angry uplifted spade-shaped head, glaring-yellow eyes. It slithers across the very plank you're standing on, three feet away, you're paralyzed, staring, too frightened to scream. Many times you've seen garter snakes, grass snakes they're

called, but this snake!—its terrible eyes fixed upon you.

An instant later, it's gone.

Already you've turned, panicked, running away. A flurry of gnats in your face and you wave wildly at them, "Oh! oh!"—blind and desperate as a small child running back up the hill, it's a considerable hill, to your great-aunt's house; the house so new to you you've never seen it before from this perspective, weatherworn and shabby with a look of anger, resentment like all such old houses that yet maintain their dignity and some measure of pretension from the street, and you're as disoriented as when you wake from a disturbing dream into a secondary dream, not knowing where you are, surrendering to pure emotion, and by the time, breathless, sweating, you're at the house, your mother has come outside to catch you in her arms. "What on earth, Josie? What's wrong with you?" Mother asks, and you tell her the snake, a long black snake, measuring with your tremulous arms the length of the snake, at least three feet long, and it seemed to be looking at *you*, as if you knew *you*, and Mother laughs, brushing at your uncombed hair with a cool hand, "Yes? Really?"

Your great-aunt Esther Allan Burkhardt,

whose house this is, and whom you'd never seen before the previous day, has come to stand in a doorway, frowning at you and Mother, arms wrapped in her apron. White as flour the apron, and her round rimless emotionless eyeglasses winking in the sun.

"That'd be a garter snake," the old woman says flatly. "They don't grow beyond ten or twelve inches and they're not dangerous that I ever heard of. You keep to yourself, miss, and they keep to themselves."

That summer I was eleven years old, my mother fled with me (as she called it) to Ransomville, New York. Where we were like poor relations in the old Burkhardt house.

"Be good while we're here, baby. Try to be good," Mother said. "We're poor as church mice, and this is the church."

There was the tacit understanding that people like us must *try to be good*: it wouldn't be natural, or easy.

The tall three-storied shingled house on Trinity Street high above the river, set back in a large, overgrown lot of aging trees, with its excess of narrow barlike windows emitting little light— the *Reverend's house* it was known in Ransomville.

Though the Reverend, Jared Burkhardt, Sr., Aunt Esther's son, a cousin of my mother's mother, had been dead for years. Like his father before him, he had been a Presbyterian minister; his church, nearby on Trinity Street, had burnt down years ago, and another, more modern church had been built for the Presbyterian congregation in a newer area of Ransomville. Reverend Burkhardt had married young and his wife too was dead, unless she was simply gone, vanished and never spoken of, at least in the *Reverend's house*. Now there lived here only Aunt Esther and her grandson Jared, Jr., a young man studying for the Presbyterian ministry at a seminary in Rochester; Jared, Jr. was home for the summer.

"At least," Mother said, "that's the story Aunt Esther tells."

"What do you mean?" I asked. "Isn't it true?"

"Stories are never 'true,'" Mother said. "But they may, almost by accident, contain 'truth.' Sometimes."

Mother would not long be interested in her Burkhardt relatives, but in these early days of our visit she was curious and inquisitive and suspicious and bemused. Her cousin-twice-removed, Jared, Sr. had been an important citizen of Ransomville, she said, but he'd died young—thirty-nine. There was some mystery about his death, some purposeful cloudiness; but asking about it, querying imperturbable old Aunt Esther for instance, would be like coaxing a stone to speak. Also, Mother suspected that there was "bad blood" between her mother's family and the Burkhardts, which would taint her, too, and even me, though we had nothing to do with any of it; and though Aunt Esther had in fact invited us to stay with her.

"'Bad blood'!—what does that mean?" I asked, revulsed by the thought, and Mother said, "'Bad feeling,' basically," and I said, "But why call it something so ugly—'bad blood'? Ugh." My throat choked up as if the smell was with us in the room. "One day," Mother said ominously, yet with satisfaction, "you'll know."

Mother calculated that Jared, Jr. was about twenty-five years old. He was a remote cousin of hers and so a yet more remote cousin of mine. It had been many years since she'd last seen him, at the Reverend's funeral, before my birth. (I did not like to think of *before my birth* and rarely asked questions pertaining to it.) She would not have recognized him, she said. "Poor Jared, Jr.!"

"Why 'poor'?" I asked.

"To be 'Jr.' is to be 'poor.' The female of the species is, at least, spared that ignominy."

Mother warned me that, though Jared was a relative of mine, that did not mean he would care to spend any time with me, nor even speak much to me. She cautioned me (obviously, Aunt Esther had instructed her in this) not to take up his time, interfere with his studies; she gathered that he'd been spending the entire summer reading theological texts and learning Hebrew. He was a religious person and it must be damned hard to be religious, Mother said, in a place like Ransomville: a country town where everyone went to church but no one much believed in God, in the sense of actually *thinking about God* more than about worldly, immediate things; *loving and worshipping God*—whatever it is that genuinely religious people give themselves up to.

"So, Josie. Keep to yourself, as Aunt Esther would say. We're here, but we're not family."

"Don't they want us here? I thought they did. The house is so *big*."

"The size of the house has little to do with the feelings of its inhabitants. Common sense should tell you that."

"Is Jared sick? Is something wrong with him?" I'd seen something in Mother's face just now.

Mother said tartly, "'Sick'?—what's 'sick'? Who is 'well'? Do you imagine, if you or I were minutely examined, we would be one hundred percent 'well'?"

When Mother spoke in this way, which was often, my anxiety grew sharper; more tactile; I could feel it flow like a low voltage electric current through me. For there was always the fear, which Mother wielded as an unspoken threat, that she would suddenly, irrevocably, *disclose too much.* She would cease to be Mother, she would slip away and I would be left alone no longer a child. For can you be a child, lacking a proximate adult to define you?

We were in the upstairs room Aunt Esther had given to Mother, an attractive though sparsely furnished room with a door opening into an adjoining, smaller room—a former nursery?—that was mine. The windows of our rooms were ridged in dust and the panes looked tear-streaked; our view was of the overgrown, rock-studded back lawn, the marsh at the bottom of the hill and the river approximately a quarter mile away. There, the beautiful Cassadaga, of which Mother had spoken so dreamily.

As Mother spoke to me of our Burkhardt relatives, now urgently, now indifferently, I had the idea that she was improvising, for her own benefit, a story of some kind; a way of organizing random facts and suppositions; once she had her Burkhardt story in place, she would know how to proceed. Often she looked me in the eye as if I were, not eleven years old, but another adult, a witness of a kind who might one day testify on her behalf. For Mother to look me in the eye in that way was exciting, yet disconcerting; for hadn't I seen her look others in the eye like that, including my father?—uttering words of apparent simplicity and directness that would turn out to be false; and the signal of the falsity, which the victim could determine only in retrospect, was that look in Delia's eye. Yet my mother was always the kind of person you chose to believe over those others incapable of lying, those luckless others who speak the truth, but a truth of a lesser significance.

I loved her so.

"Why are we here, Mother, where people don't want us?" I asked, clutching at Mother's arm. "Can't we go somewhere else? *Can't we go back home?*"

Deliberately Mother disengaged my warm sticky fingers from her cool, delicately boned wrist. She was only half-dressed, in one of her creamy-lacy slips, and her hair was unbrushed, untidy. "Think of Ransomville and the *Reverend's house* as home, baby. You won't have any trouble with definitions, then."

"But aren't we ever going back.... there? To . . ."

Deftly Mother cut me off, before I could utter the forbidden words *Dad, Daddy, Father*. If one is going to make a break, Mother said, the break must be absolute, and no looking back.

Mother said, her gaze on me calculating, impatient, of the silver glint of light reflected in swift-moving water, "There is no 'there,' there is only 'here.' Just as there is no 'then,' but only 'now.' America is founded upon such principles, and, as Americans, we must be, too."

Mother stretched luxuriant as a big cat. She stood above me, beginning to brush her hair—thick, sun-bleached, wheat-colored hair—that fell to her shoulders. She was *Delia S*——— and she was thirty-one years old and she was a married woman who had abruptly left her husband for reasons known only to her: I knew these facts, but I did not know who my mother was. And what would it mean to be thirty-one years old—an unthinkable age! Still less did I know if it was a common act for a wife and mother to leave her husband, or if this was a uniqueness of Delia's own. In the cities in which we'd lived I had come to have some knowledge of other children's mothers but in my pride I did not believe that such knowledge applied to Delia S——.

I was saying to Mother, I didn't know why exactly, *the black snake, the black snake, beautiful, those eyes!* in a small hurt voice, "Mother, I guess I'm . . . afraid," and Mother looked at me in exasperation, "Don't be silly: 'afraid' is only a word," and I stammered, ". . . afraid of . . ." and Mother said, "'Afraid' is only a word, a mere exhalation of air. Don't utter it to yourself and it won't be. 'Af-fraiiid.'" She was pursing her lips ironically, meaning to ridicule. And it was right for her to ridicule me when, in such states, I seemed scarcely my age but far younger, purposefully childish. But suddenly I began to cry, pounded my fists on her bed, the bed's aged springs creaked in protest and I pounded harder and kicked. Mother had chided me many times in the past about surrendering to the mere ghosts of sound that are words and now I shouted, "I hate you! What is there that isn't a *word!* That isn't a *sound!* Whatever it is . . . 'af-fraiiid' . . . *that's what I am.*"

"Really, Josie! To take yourself so seriously, at your age," Mother said coolly. "An eleven-year-old scarcely exists."

A red mist passed over my brain. "I *exist*, God damn! *I'm here!*"

To my horror then Mother, smiling her lovely mocking smile, her slender shoulders lifted in a shrug, seemed to ease into a blinding swath of sunshine that poured through the latticed windowpanes like liquid flame; or did she disappear—dissolve—into a parabola of a mirror attached by an antiquated tarnished frame to the back of a closet door. My vision was blinded by hot raging tears; I wept, choked, kicked, looked up, looked up squinting in dread. *Mother was gone.*

You would not call it love you would have another name, another word for it.

Shutting my eyes sometimes to the point of dizziness, vertigo. To the point of an almost unbearable excitation and dread. And I see him, my cousin Jared, Jr. So many years later. I see him as an upright flame, a figure and not a person. If I try to summon back his face, the sound of his voice, and the sensation in my stomach like a key turning in a lock when he touched me, I lose everything.

* * *

The Great Perennial Question. That summer we came
to live in the *Reverend's house* where we would stay
for eighteen months. Where we'd lived before,
and with whom; where we'd driven in haste in
Mother's second-hand '57 Plymouth filled with
our few suitcases, cardboard boxes, folded items
of clothing—that became a name, a word, unspoken. Mother would never again allude to it,
and by degrees I began to forget for *whatever is unspoken is soon unknown.* Nor did Aunt Esther make in-
quiries. She was a stiff-girdled woman with a
face that appeared polished like one of the
gleaming newel posts of the household, her
small pebble-colored eyes shrewd behind polished lenses. Her strawlike ashy-white hair fitted
in thin permed crimps over her scalp and it was
difficult to tell when she wore a hairnet and
when not, or if Aunt Esther's hairnet was in fact
her hair, so perfectly meshed was net with hair.
Her old-woman's flesh had an angry compact-
ness that spilled out where it could—flaccid upper arms, swollen ankles, drooping chins. Esther
Allan Burkhardt was a proud keeper of the *Reverend's house* to which a few aging neighbors came
dutifully, as well as, now and then, the current
minister of the First Presbyterian Church of Ran-

somville and his wife; in her role as the *Reverend's widow* she wore costumes of the darker sere hues, shapeless matronly dresses with swaths of useless fabric at the hips, primly cloth-covered buttons the size of half-dollars; over these dresses, she wore aprons of blinding whiteness. She was both bustling and fiercely elegiac. When she smiled, you could hear papery skin stretch. "So good to see you after so many years, Delia. And . . ." her glance wandering to me as I stood awkward-armed, beside Mother, ". . . your daughter." A moment's pause then, as if she'd forgotten my name.

The center of Aunt Esther's life was her grandson, Jared, Jr.

In that somber house on Trinity Street where, even at midday in some of the rooms, it was dusk, an atmosphere of *waitfulness* prevailed— but for what? Sometimes it seemed to me I could hear muffled murmurous voices, whispers. When, the first week of our visit, I laughed at a droll remark of my mother's uttered just out of hearing of Aunt Esther, the sound was jarring, like breaking glass.

At a distance, through a maze of part-opened doors, reflected in mirrors and polished surfaces the figure of Jared, Jr. glided. I would see him by chance, a tall thin retreating figure, head turned from me as if he suspected, and resented, my watching for him; always he was carrying a book or books. He ate most of his meals alone in the rooms on the first floor of the house that were "Jared's quarters." Occasionally he could be persuaded by his doting grandmother to have breakfast with her in the formal dining room and if Mother and I appeared Aunt Esther rose hastily from the table to head us off. "Yes? Up so early?" Mother and I knew to have our breakfasts in the kitchen.

Laughingly Mother whispered in my ear as she banged about in the dreary, old-fashioned kitchen, "As if we would want to sit down with *them*!"

Slyly I would push the swinging door to the dining room open a fraction of an inch to spy on my cousin. A boyish young man in oddly formal clothes, with a head that looked too large for his narrow shoulders, a beaky profile, skin the drab rubbed-out hue of pencil erasures on paper. At the table he sat oblivious of his surroundings, a strange mixture of humility and hauteur as his grandmother maintained a continuous stream of solicitous, vaguely chiding chatter to which he appeared politely to listen even as he made notations in the margins of a book propped up before him. His elbows framed an exquisite bone-china plate upon which eggs, Canadian bacon, toast cooled, scarcely touched.

Fresh every morning was a perfectly starched and ironed long-sleeved white shirt for Jared, Jr. the seminary student. Even if, most days, he hid away in his part of the house amid his books. If he left the house, on foot to stroll to the small public library in town, or by car to drive away, gone at times for much of a day, he never failed to wear a tie and coat. Jared walked with a self-conscious posture, head high, shoulders back as if someone had just nudged him *Stand straight, boy!* Mother said of him, "Poor Jared! He has a certain destiny. You can see it in some of the Burkhardts. It's inherited from his father, and probably from his grandfather who was a Presbyterian minister, too. 'Men of God' they used to call such men. Lucky for us, there never have been any 'women of God.'"

I asked Mother if she remembered Jared's father *the Reverend*, and Mother said, "If I said I did? What would that mean? Nothing is so notorious as human memory, Josie. Brain cells are ninety-nine percent saline solution—it's a miracle we remember anything at all. Neurons are forever

discharging, synapses are being severed like rotting twine. It's believed that brain activity is electricity flashing like lightning in one area of the cortex, then another. You know how idiosyncratic lightning is. You can't track it, predict it. A blink of an eyelid, you'd halfway expect everything in human memory to be erased. When a person says, 'Oh yes, I remember,' be sure that he or she is already inventing. The instinct to tell tales is located in the same part of the medulla as the instinct to reproduce the species. So even if I did recall Reverend Jared Burkardt, Sr., whom I'd seen only once before his death, and who was, in his coffin, an eerily handsome corpse with an ivory-pale face, it would be only the mere outward husk of the man, not the inner, secret man. With such personalities as Jared, Sr. and Jared, Jr. it's only the inner man that is real. The other is just a flimsy impression on the optic nerve."

I asked Mother if that could be true for us, too? — We were just impressions on others' optic nerves?

"Usually, yes." Mother was in one of her airy, incandescent moods. Critically examining herself before the full-length mirror, holding up to herself dresses, silky little suits, ruffled blouses.

It was the first morning of her new job—receptionist, at Ransomville's leading real estate company—which she'd been offered, evidently, without an interview, having simply met the company's owner in town the previous week, and struck up a conversation with him on the embankment of the Cassadaga. "That's why it's necessary, Josie, to control that optic impression. Especially if you're a woman."

But I'm not a woman! I wanted to scream at Mother.

Long ago, in my infancy, Delia and I were near-equals (for power resides in ruthless, unquestioned self-centeredness); with time, as I'd grown, becoming less and less a child, I'd lost my power, surrendering it to my mother. For she was herself a child, deceptive and fascinating in her enticements to make you love her, and to cause you to want, oh so yearningly!—for her to love you. *Which could never be, not in the way you desire.*

At last Mother chose a silky little suit with a snug-fitting jacket and flared skirt, snowdrop checks against a navy-blue background; with swift-flying practiced hands she bound up her lavish hair, into a chignon; forced her stockinged feet, which were slender, but rather long, into stylish high-heeled shoes. Before I could protest, or complain that I was sad, lonely, frightened of being left alone in the *Reverend's house*, there came a hurried damp kiss carelessly pressed against my cheek, and Mother was gone.

That afternoon for the first time daring to venture into the room downstairs off the parlor, the room called by Aunt Esther the library; her son Jared, Sr.'s library; a place of somber sepia shadows, mildew odors, faint tobacco smoke. Aged books with badly cracked spines like misshapen human figures were crowded onto shelves reaching to the ceiling. It was that magical hour between three and four, when, I'd already discovered, Aunt Esther disappeared into her bedroom for a nap. And I'd seen Jared, Jr. walk off in the direction of town, in white shirt, tie, coat, slowly, with a pinched gait, head bowed as if, from behind glasses that resembled his grandmother's, his eyes restlessly searched the sidewalk before him.

Overgrown junipers so obscured the downstairs windows of this part of the house, it might have been dusk.

Jared, Jr. often studied in his father's library. I saw that he had neatly cleared a space for himself at his father's desk, which was a large, heavy piece of furniture with numerous shelves and drawers; he'd brought a cushion to place in the well-worn hollow of his father's old swivel chair; there were a half-dozen newly sharpened pencils, bright yellow, of the kind I saw him turn compulsively between his fingers at breakfast, arranged on the desktop. The library was airless, I began to feel slightly dizzy. On my heel turning slowly, seeing what Jared, Jr. would be seeing if in his swivel chair he turned, in a slow revolution. Books, books! But on the walls were numerous reproductions of Jesus Christ. The wise eyes, the dark beard and moustache, dark longish hair. In some reproductions, a halo glowed faintly about Jesus Christ's head but in others there was none. In some, Jesus Christ wore His crown of spikes and blood glistened on His forehead; already He was stretched upon his cross, spikes piercing His hands and feet. Yet in other depictions He was preaching to the multitudes, in glowing magisterial garments. He was a pale, sorrowful, womanly figure. He was a swarthy-skinned, robust, muscular figure. He was gentle-eyed, He was belligerent. In one, His head and shoulders appeared to have been formed by hundreds of tiny pieces of colored glass — "The Savior Jesus," a twelfth-century mosaic from Madrid, Spain. Another head and shoulders was of a rapturous, dreamy Jesus Christ, a starburst of light behind Him — "The Redeemer of Man," sixteenth-century Bologna, Italy. There was a strangely square-jawed, heavy-browed, short-haired Jesus Christ, very dark-skinned, undated, from Northern Africa; there was the familiar "Head of Christ," honey-skinned, pretty, dated 1940. There was the triumphant Jesus Christ, robed, wearing an elaborate Arabian headdress, depicted in the midst of one of His miracles — "The Raising of Jarius' Daughter," Germany, 1861. (Jarius' daughter was about my age, and very blond.) I looked from one Jesus Christ to the other, turning on my heel in bewilderment and growing alarm, for which *was* the Son of God? — which were the imposters? Why had Reverend Burkhardt, who must have known which Jesus Christ was the true savior, honored the others, the false saviors, by putting their likenesses on his library wall? There could be only one Jesus Christ, after all.

I wondered if Jared, Jr. Felt such dizziness, such shortness of breath, contemplating these walls.

The titles of books flew at me now — *A History of the Old Testament, The Story of the Gospels, Jesus of*

Nazareth, *The Secret of the Dead Sea Scrolls, The Miracles of Jesus Christ, An Atlas of the Ancient World, The Settlements of the Descendants of Noah, The Twelve Tribes of Canaan.* On the desk, at a careless angle, as if it had been shoved away, was one of the aged, broken-spined books, *The Great Perennial Question: Who Was Jesus?*

The first time you see him in the secret place the sun is beating down from above so hard you imagine an opened, panting mouth. You've slipped away to the marsh, to the riverbank. Believing yourself alone. Here in Ransomville, in the dead heat of August, you're always alone. But there he is — shirtless, his back to you, looking out over the river. He's lying motionless on the riverbank, on his elbows. His longish hair in damp tendrils at the nape of his neck. Thick dark hair the color of smoke, threaded with silvery-gray. How skinny he is! — the vertebrae of his spine prominent as tiny knuckles, a ripply impress of ribs through his translucent-pale skin. *Run away! Go back to the house!* It's a bright blazing August afternoon, the sun glitters on the river like a serpent's scales.

But you stand paralyzed on the rotted plank set in marshy earth. Beyond the straggly stand of bamboo, the spiky marsh grasses that grow to a height of five feet. Out of sight of the house above.

"Girl!"

The voice is a boy's voice, but commanding. It seems to come from all sides and beneath it, humming, murmuring, like a great pulse, the river's sound.

"Girl, I know you're here. Show yourself."

Slowly, teasingly turning, brushing a strand of languid hair out of his eyes, your cousin Jared sees you, and frowns instead of smiling. *Now you can't escape: he has you.* Without his glasses, his eyes are enlarged. In them, twin coronas burn like distant suns.

In Ransomville boys go without shirts, it's a common sight. Rough shouting boys on bicycles, boys who trample the riverbank nearer town, dark-tanned, boisterous. But Jared is so different. Jared isn't a boy at all, but a man. He sits up now, elbows on his knees. His chest is pale, slightly concave. Gleaming with molecules of perspiration. Dark hairs on his skin like smudges made with a dirty thumb, and the surprise of his hard-looking little nipples! — you look away, embarrassed.

"What's wrong, girl? Cat got your tongue?"

Jared has neatly folded his perfectly starched and ironed white long-sleeved shirt and laid it beside him on the ground. He has removed his shoes and socks as well—his feet are long, narrow, bluish-white, toes twitching. He regards you sidelong, now smiling.

"Girl, you've been following me, haven't you? Spying on me?"

You would turn and run back to the house but you can't, you can only come forward. A breathless din on all sides of cicadas, bullfrogs. The raw melancholy cries of red-winged blackbirds CA-CA-CA-C*A*! CA-CA-CA-CA-C*A*! You're shaking your head *no!*—you haven't been spying on Jared—but a powerful heat rises from the ground, rushes up your body and into your face. Jared laughs and signals for you to come closer. Beside him on the riverbank, here. Where no one can see.

"How did you know I was here, then? Eh?"

"I . . . didn't know."

"*Didn't?* Then why are you here?"

Close up, Jared's face is a young-old face, his forehead creased with thinking, little nicks and dents in his gaunt cheeks. In his eyes those twin coronas, burning. A fever-sweaty smell lifts from him as he moves his arms, shrugs his bony shoulders. He's teasing the way Mother does sometimes, you can't know, is he serious or just testing you.

Jared says, more gently, "I brought you here with my thoughts, Josie. That's why you're here."

You shake your head, trying to laugh. "You can't do that."

"What? What can't I do?"

" . . . bring me here, with . . . your thoughts."

"Oh yes, I can. I can do all sorts of things with my thoughts."

Jared laughs, the first time you've heard him laugh, a high-pitched boyish laughter that fades almost at once. The kind of laughter that entices you to join in, helpless as if you're being tickled, but then almost at once it's gone. You see that Jared has closed his fingers around your left wrist. In reflex your arm twitches, you want to wrench away, scramble to your feet like a panicked cat and run back to the house. But you can't. Paralyzed trembling on your knees beside your cousin Jared who is on his knees now, too, looming over you. His wavering head, thick smoke-colored hair, burning eyes. He is speaking quietly, with authority. "You don't remember the first time you saw me, Josie. But I remember the first time I saw you."

You shake your head, confused. You hope Jared will be kind to you, won't hurt you.

"Don't you remember, girl? Try."

"I . . . don't know."

"Speak up, I can't hear you. Is that the way you speak, at school? You'll be mistaken for retarded. You'll be misdiagnosed. Do you know what a fate it can be, to be *misdiagnosed?*" Jared smiles strangely, no mirth in his eyes. His teeth are small, child-sized, rather grayish, crowded in his narrow jaws. "The instinct among our species for making premature judgments, 'assessing' and 'cataloguing' and 'predicting' is a terrible one, it can ruin lives. We must seize control when we can. That's what I've done." He pauses, and his fingers circling your wrist tighten, in emphasis. "You don't remember the first time you saw me, Josie, do you? Here in the marsh?"

"In the . . . marsh?"

"Yes. Here in the marsh." Jared smiles slyly, tugging at your wrist. "You ran away screaming like a silly little girl."

The black snake. He means the black snake.

"Why'd you run away screaming, like a silly little girl? Is that what you are, a silly little girl?"

You want to protest but Jared takes hold of your chin, holds your head still; stares into your eyes as no one has ever stared into your eyes; you feel the sun pouring into you, dissolving your bones. He asks in a low, insistent, hypnotic voice *Are you a silly little girl? Are you a silly little girl?* and you try to shake your head no! No I'm not.

Jared releases you, now brushing your damp hair from your forehead with his thumbs. Mirthful quivers run through him, you can feel his superior heartbeat pounding at your temples. He says, chiding, "Next time you see me here in the marsh, Josie, don't be afraid. Remember, I would never hurt *you*. We're blood kin, we understand each other. The first glimpse I had of you, though you pretended to be terrified of me, I *knew*."

The din of summer insects, cries of birds. Across the sluggish-sullen river, swarms of gnats like toxic gases wavering in your vision.

You're stammering, "I . . . don't believe you! You couldn't be a . . . "

"A what?"

" . . . snake." Your voice falters, shy as if you're uttering a forbidden word.

Slyly Jared laughs, scratching at his chest. Running a forefinger over one of his berrylike little nipples. "I couldn't? I, Jared Burkhardt, Jr.?"

You shake your head no, you hear yourself laughing, frightened, though you know that what Jared says must be true.

Must be true, you know.

For how otherwise did he know about the long black snake, the snake's glaring-yellow eyes fixed on *you*.

Roughly now Jared tugs you to your feet. You're panicked where he will take you, but you can't struggle free. Through the bamboo stalks you see the tall pewter-shingled house above, how many hundreds of yards away, on the far side of the marsh—the windows blinking opaque in the sun. You think, *If Mother is watching! If Mother is there!* But it's a weekday afternoon, Mother is elsewhere. No one is there.

In the bleached-out sky there's a surprise: a faint sickle moon.

Jared hauls you farther down the bank, to the edge of the river. His bare feet sinking in the pebbly-clay soil. You think *He won't hurt me, he likes me. He is my cousin. Blood kin.* Across the river there is junglelike vegetation, the rears of houses and buildings at a distance, to the east, toward the small downtown of Ransomville, there's a bridge, much too far away for anyone to see you should anyone be looking, should anyone care. To the west, the river winds out of sight beyond wooded hills. How alone you are, you and your cousin Jared!

You ask Jared how can there be a moon in the sky in daytime, like a nervous schoolgirl you giggle asking your question and Jared glances skyward and says, matter-of-fact as a school teacher, "All the moons and suns and stars of the universe are, in theory, 'in' the sky at all times, even if you can't see them; even, in a sense, if they've burnt out and become extinct. Just because you can't see something hardly means it doesn't exist."

Along the edge of the languid water we move, feet sinking in the soft soil. Birds scatter in exaggerated alarm out of the underbrush on shore and reel, on flapping wings, over the river. Blackbirds, swifts, a single snowy egret, brilliant white feathers like something dabbed onto the riverscape with a brush. You pass through a cloud of gnats. Mosquitoes whine in your ears. Jared's fingers looping your wrist tight, unrelenting. You're out of breath, half-sobbing. Jared doesn't look back, pulling you along.

Don't provoke him, don't anger. Don't ever.

At last beneath a ruin of an old two-lane bridge about a mile from your great-aunt's house, Jared ceases running and pulls you down into a crouch with him. Is this a game? Are you hiding from someone? He signals for you to be quiet, he mimes placing the palm of his hand over your mouth in warning. *No, no! Josie will be good.* The feverish, sweaty smell of Jared's pale-glimmering body makes your nostrils pinch. His dark eyes are rimmed with flame, his pulse beats accelerated in your veins. "Quiet. Quiet. Quiet. Quiet," he's murmuring rhythmically, hypnotically. You're so frightened it's hard to see where you are. You have an impression of toppled, rusted iron girders, great slabs of concrete broken and cracked like an ancient landscape. In the river bed are boulders bleached white by the sun, encrusted with dried moss like mucus. There is a shallow, sheltered pool beneath the bridge, formed by fallen debris; a secret place, it seems, in deep, airless shadow; out of the white-glazed sunshine and the open river and sky. Somewhere above, teasingly near yet invisible, like wakefulness at the edge of a dream, an occasional car or truck passes on a road. "Don't hurt me! Oh please . . . " You hear yourself begging, but Jared pays no heed. Slowly and ceremoniously, his fingers uncertain at first, he undresses you—pulling your sleeveless t-shirt off over your head, tugging down your cotton shorts, nylon panties. You've begun to sob but Jared speaks gently, compassionately. "Girl, you're not very clean, are you? Your slut of a mother doesn't have time for you, eh? *But I do.*"

Playful, but urgent, smiling hard as he scoops up handfuls of water to spill onto you, your heated face, neck, flat goose-pimpled little breasts, belly, and shrinking buttocks. It might be a game, and nothing more serious — you're squealing, giggling, Jared is tickling you while seeming not to know what he does, unless in fact he knows, and his pretense of not-knowing is part of the game.

Stooping then to splash water onto his own face, water running in rivulets down his fine-frizzed chest, down his pale, gleaming back. Murmuring how it's necessary *to be clean, to be clean, to be clean.* His breath coming short, excited. Even when he releases you now you crouch motionless, paralyzed. You no more think of running from him than you might think of wading out desperately into the water, swimming to the farther shore. Nor would you think of screaming, the highway is too far away and maybe there is no highway, no one passing by to help you. Jared says you're *a good girl, good girl, good girl.* He's groping for something in the pebbly soil, finds what he wants — a broken shell, a clam shell the size of an ear, beautiful iridescent mother-ofpearl sheen of the interior though the outside is coarse and dirty like most river shells. He lifts it bringing its sharp edge against your breast-bone and you wince, he relents, presses the edge against his own breastbone until a half-moon of bright blood springs out. He brings your fingertips to the blood, then lifts them to his lips, to lick them; then to your lips, and you lick the blood, too. You're laughing, your head swims. Jared laughs, too. He's pleased with you, he likes you, won't hurt you. Though bringing the razor-sharp edge of the shell again to your breast-bone, between your little breasts, and again pressing, pressing—and this time you cry, "Oh!" as the blood springs out and runs down your chest. And Jared holds you tight murmuring *good girl, good girl* touching the seeping blood, licking his fingertips then forcing them into your mouth, too. You almost gag, but don't.

"Now we know each other, eh, Josie? True blood kin. Now we are each other's secret."

An eyelid's blink, and all memory is erased.

When next we encountered each other, in the house. There was, the following day, Jared, Jr. just en-

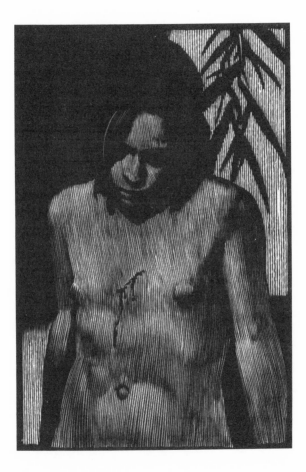

tering the library downstairs, carrying a Bible, a notebook, slightly disheveled hair as if he'd been running his hands through it, head bowed and lower lip protruding in vexing-brooding thought. Jared, Jr. so handsome!—in his perfectly starched and ironed white long-sleeved shirt, a boy-minister!—so handsome with even his gaunt cheeks and graying hair and shadowed eyes that did not so much swerve from me, and from Mother, to avoid us, as they were simply not aware of us at all.

As lost in a waking dream as I was to be increasingly in the weeks and months to come in Ransomville in the *Reverend's house,* I was often not aware of others (including sometimes Mother herself!) though staring open-eyed at them.

Each other's secret.

It seemed appropriate that, in his grandmother's house, Jared, Jr. scarcely acknowledged me. He was twenty-five, I was eleven years old. He was closer to Mother's age than to mine, yet rarely would he exchange more than a few murmured words with her; all the effort was on Mother's side. For a beautiful woman, so confident of her attractiveness to men that it did not surprise her when a man followed her in the street, or contrived an ingenious means of being introduced to her, Mother was distinctly annoyed that her cousin Jared, Jr. was so seemingly indifferent to her. In my ear she whispered, even as Jared was shutting a door against us, "Isn't he strange, Josie! Our kinsman 'Jared, Jr.'"

I nodded vaguely, my eyes slide away sideways like silver minnows.

There were silver minnows, tiny crabs, miniature clam shells in the pool of river water beneath the ruined bridge.

When we were alone, Mother spoke irritably of Jared, and at length. She was a woman of theories, plots. It was her belief that all about us, invisible as radio waves, are *plots*: partial, groping stories in the process of being invented, of which we must be alert, always; which we must try to decode, and, if necessary, for our own survival, circumvent. The story of Mother's marriage, the years of her wifehood, motherhood, etc.—she'd simply taken control of the trajectory of that plot, wrested it from another and claimed it for her own. She had brought it to THE END. (In fact, was Mother divorced from the man she no longer referred to as *your father?* I was not kept informed on such adult subjects and dared not inquire. Of course I looked through the mail that came for Mother, dropped through the slightly tarnished brass mail-slot in the foyer, but few letters came.)

Mother said, "There's something unnatural and uncanny about Jared, isn't there? He seems not to have any friends in Ransomville, though he grew up here. Aunt Esther says he 'doesn't mingle.' The way she says it, it's like Jared doesn't mingle with the local *dogs*. The family's hope for him, she says, is that he'll be ordained a minister like his father, and return to Ransomville as the minister here, in the 'new' church. I wonder what the present minister, and his congregation, think of that! Ministers and priests go where they are assigned by their superiors, I happen to know. Of course, money might be involved. I wouldn't doubt that." Mother paused, for a moment wistful: *money* evoked subterranean emotions in her, though she would not pursue them in my presence. "Poor Jared! I don't wonder he was sent home from the seminary last spring, as people say in town. No one knows why, exactly — 'nervous collapse' is just *words*. Are nerves tiny bones, or toothpicks, that can literally *collapse?* And, if so, how are they repaired? It might be like electrical wiring — these old houses are notorious for faulty wiring." Mother laughed cruelly, and rapped her knuckles against her own head, for emphasis. "There's a mystery about Jared, I'm convinced. If I didn't have my own life, and my own . . . " Mother paused, for perhaps she meant to say *mystery*, or *plot*; I understood that she was involved with a new man, very likely her employer Mr. Drayton of Drayton Realty, Inc., though all of this was strictly secret from me of course, " . . . well, I don't have time. I asked Aunt Esther if Jared would be returning to the seminary next month and the poor woman positively stammered, didn't know how to reply. Jared's problem, in my opinion, is that he takes himself too seriously. A 'theological seminary' is an institution in which, in actual fact, a nonexisting object — 'God' — is studied. Of course, you'd have a nervous collapse in such a place. Obviously, Jared isn't well. If you look at those eyes of his . . . !" Mother shuddered, deliciously.

Each other's secret. Blood kin.

Good girl, good girl. Good . . .

I resented Mother speaking so familiarly of Jared. She did not know Jared, at all. It was not her privilege to know Jared. My heart pounded sullenly in defiance of her.

Sharp-eyed Mother noted my expression, and pinched me.

"What do you mean, miss, by that bulldog look?"

I shook my head quickly, guiltily. "Nothing, Mother."

"Yes? What are you thinking, that you don't want your own mother to know?"

"T-Thinking? Nothing . . . "

My face burned, my words tripped over one another as if there were pebbles in my mouth. Mother seized a strand of my limp, curly hair and gave it a twist. Teasing of course, and *teasing* allowed her, as if by accident, to make me wince.

Mother said, her eyes glaring splendidly, "*Is* it possible to think of 'nothing'? Isn't that a logical impossibility?"

"I . . . don't know . . . "

"For a person of at least minimal intelligence, of course it is. And we both know, from the difficulties you've had with your ridiculous teachers, who expect you to be just a little less stupid than they are themselves, that you're of exceptionally high intelligence. Consider: to say you're thinking of 'nothing'—to stammer such a flimsy excuse—is certainly to have thought of 'something.' There is the 'something' that is in the mind, and there is the 'nothing' that is the verbal screen for it. A screen meant to hide and to deceive, yes?"

I shook my head, frightened. I was blinking rapidly so that Mother could not see my eyes.

"Is it something about Jared? You haven't been bothering him, have you?"

"No . . ."

"Haven't been prowling about his rooms, have you? Going through his things?"

"No."

"What, then?"

Mother had taken hold of my skinny shoulders with her talon fingers. Her accusing eyes that were a pale bluish-gray, flecked with tiny near-invisible mica chips like certain of the stones, the beautiful stones scattered along the shore of the Cassadaga, boring into mine. Those eyes that claimed *You can't hide from me! Can't keep any secrets from me!*

For there must be a day — an hour, a minute! — when for the first time in its life a baby tries to deceive its mother; a moment when what we call will is first exerted; the instinctive, improvised gesture of deception, subterfuge that will become an integral part of one's mental life. Could a parent detect such a moment, it's possible that he or she could so stifle it that the baby's *plot* is forever circumvented. In seizing me as she did at such times, knowing I dared not resist, Mother meant to evoke the magical time before that time when she was, not simply Mother, now known to me, too, as *Delia S*———, but, to me, *all that was*. But I could elude her now, brazenly looking her in the eyes. Her beautiful eyes.

Stumbling and faltering, tears glistening, I told Mother about having poked about in the library, while Aunt Esther was having her nap the other day. I told her about the numerous Jesus Christs, *The Great Perennial Question*. I told her it frightened me, that grown-ups should not *know, know for certain*, who Jesus Christ was.

"All right, then," Mother said, losing interest at once, and releasing me. "If that's all. Poking about in that dreary old library among my uncle's old things . . . " Mother shrugged, catching a glimpse of herself in a mirror; tidying a strand of radiantly brown-blown hair at the nape of her neck. *A daughter of mine!* she seemed to be saying, winking at the lovely reflection that floated before her.

The Reverend's house on Trinity Street, Ransomville. A street of fairly large, prosperous-looking houses. Most of them built in the late 1800s, like the *Reverend's house* which was built, according to a date I discovered in the stone foundation, in 1893. There was, farther up Trinity Street, the Trinity Episcopal Church a few blocks away; there had been, close by the *Reverend's house*, the First Presbyterian Church of Ransomville. (The brick and mortar ruins of the old church still remained, amid a vacant lot of wildly flourishing young trees, shrubs and weeds; I'd several times explored it, alone, carrying a stick to ward off rats, snakes.) On Trinity Street there lived, as Aunt Esther liked to boast, the *very best citizens* of Ransomville. By which she meant of course the *most well-to-do*. Across from us was a red-brick Georgian mansion owned by a district judge; next door, a Greek Revival monstrosity owned by Mr. Perkins of Perkins Trust; on the other side, a stately, weatherworn white colonial owned by Mr. Endicott, the heir of Endicott Mills. The minister of Trinity Episcopal lived in a handsome fieldstone rectory beside his church, and the current mayor of Ransomville—who'd been mayor, in fact, for the past fifteen years—lived in a Victorian house that resembled Aunt Esther's, tall, narrow, somber, with dark shingles and steep roofs. At the rear of Trinity, the land fell roughly away, sloping to the Cassadaga River a quarter mile below. Here was the marsh, a place of brackish odors, rich rot-

ting intoxicating odors that wafted up, on airless late-summer nights, to my room. Along the
river's shore was a wild profusion of bamboo,
rushes, cattails; poplars and weeping willows;
nameless gnarled and thorny shrubs with stony
red berries, bitter on the tongue. Already by
early autumn the sumac began to turn flame-
red. Aunt Esther spoke disapprovingly of me
prowling about the river as she called it *like common
children, white trash. Not a place for a girl her age to go
alone.*

Trinity Street was Ransomville's premier
street. At least at its northern end. Elsewhere,
it intersected with Washburn, Mt. Rose, Chip-
pewa, streets and neighborhoods designated by
Aunt Esther as *changing,* or *mixed.* As Mt. Rose de-
scended to the river, past the old Presbyterian
cemetery, crossing the railroad tracks that ran
parallel to the river, its pavement grew cracked
and potholed; there were stretches of uncul-
tivated land, interspersed with rickety woodframe houses, trailers on cement blocks, tar-
paper shanties. Here were the families of *poor
whites* and *coloreds.* Grassless yards in which mon-
grel dogs barked and howled, goats were teth-
ered, chickens ran loose. Junked hulks of once-
gaudy autos still FOR SALE. Toppled trees, rotted

limbs—debris from winter storm damage going back for years. Beside one sprawling ramshackle house near the railroad yard, which I bicycled past on my way to the public library on Main Street, though in fact it was several blocks out of my way, was a half-acre lot in which two horses, a mule, four goats, and, in a corner, a sow and numerous piglets were kept—the pigs were wonderfully ugly, brown-speckled, with gnomish-pug faces and red-rimmed, crafty eyes.

The bicycle was an old, fenderless, rust-stippled Schwinn. A boy's bike with a crossbar. It had once belonged to Jared, Jr. when he'd been a boy. Jared offered it to me—*a secret gift, an exchange*—though it was to have been my idea, having discovered the bike in the garage, thick with dust, unused for years.

Jared warned that certain things between us must remain secrets from my mother and from his grandmother. *If you tell, girl, I can't prevent what might happen.*

The Burkhardts had been early settlers of Ransomville, having pushed on westward through Massachusetts in the early 1800s. They'd owned farmland surrounding the town, and they'd invested in the Chautauqua & Buffalo Railroad that bisected the town, north and south, linking it with the small cities of Derby, Yewville, Chautauqua Falls. It was Mother's belief that railroad money, or what remained of it, must be what maintained the *Reverend's house* and its occupants at the present time. Though dividends must be modest, or Aunt Esther would have kept the house in better repair. She would not have been so concerned with her niece Delia S——— paying "her share" of household expenses and her great-niece eleven-year-old Josie doing "her share" of household chores.

"The Burkhardts were always proud people, and the pride in this house," Mother said, wrinkling her nose peevishly, "is wearing thin. Like a mirror—like most of the mirrors, here—where the lead backing has begun to corrode through the glass."

I asked Mother what had become of Jared's mother. Was she still alive or was she dead, like his father?

"Dead, probably," Mother said, with a sigh. "Poor woman! By this time, I'd think there wouldn't be much alternative for her."

If you entered the marsh you surrendered your body. You were not yourself, your name was *you, she,* girl. There were whispery sucking noises. There were frogs' grunts. Like a man's grunts, they were—you'd heard men grunting and wheezing, wheezing and grunting, long ago when you weren't meant to hear. You knew what it was even then: the animal pulp inside forcing its way out. Oozing, bubbling, shooting its way out.

Good girl! But now you must be cleansed. Jared briskly washed your sticky fingers in the river, Jared splashed water onto your sweaty-sticky face. You wanted to say *I love you, Jared* but he gripped you by the back of the neck and lowered your face to the water that tasted metallic, bitter. Until you gasped, flailed your silly arms like a drowning goose and he took pity on you. *Oh for God's sake: Nobody's going to kill you, why would anyone care to kill you?*

Josie S———'s household chores. Mowing the lawn where, in scattered patches, it was still grassy. (The shade from the oaks and chestnuts was so deep, most of the grass had died out. And where it had survived it was choked with crabgrass and dandelion, damned hard to push a hand mower through.) Helping the *cleaning lady* as Aunt Esther called her, a stout yellow-skinned person with rheumy, resentful eyes and a sour beery breath who came, always late, Monday and Thursday mornings. (One of my tasks was ironing. But I was allowed to iron only flat boring things like napkins, towels, sheets; the methodical ironing of Jared's dazzling white shirts, which I yearned to do, was reserved for Aunt Esther, herself.) Helping in the kitchen with food preparation, cooking, clean-up. (In theory, Mother and I were supposed to work together in the kitchen most evenings. In fact, Mother rarely ate at home since she was *taken out for dinner* as she spoke of it casually and often did not return to the house by midnight even on weekdays. So most of the kitchen chores fell to me. Unless, as sometimes happened, to my surprise, out of loneliness I guess Aunt Esther joined me. "Well. Just you and me, Josie. Better than nothing, I suppose!"

If once you start you might not be able to stop. With a cash bonus of $500 from her employer, Mr. Drayton, for her first month's work, Delia S——— went on a *shopping spree* just after Labor Day — "A 'shopping spree' is what women have traditionally enjoyed doing with their time, and what men enjoy seeing them do. At least, certain combinations of men and women." Mother's bemused tone did not match the enthusiasm with which she spent money not her own on clothes for herself and me; especially on those occasions when she was buying new clothes and school supplies for me. The new school year, in a new town—how exciting! She did not look at me too closely, smiling her radiant smile. Drove us to Chautauqua Falls for a Saturday's shopping in three or four "good" stores and it would have been a happy occasion except: helping me, against my wishes, pull a dress over my head in a changing room, she discovered the *wounds.* Cuts, scratches, bruises. The sickle-shaped cut on my chest was nearly healed, its scab ready to fall off; others, protected by bandaids, were only a few days' old. On my belly, below my belly button, there was a rough reddened patch that looked as if it had been made by sandpaper or the unhoned edge of a knife. Mother was incensed, appalled, as if she'd discovered these blemishes on her own flawless skin. Crying, "Oh Josie! What on earth happened to you?" and I said stammering I'd fallen down at the river I guessed, stumbling over rocks, and Mother said, "But how can you be so clumsy? A girl your age—almost twelve— isn't a *child.*" Quickly yet evening I said, for I had only to calm myself to hear Jared's stern admonition *Always think before you speak: think of me,* that I guessed I'd fallen off my bicycle, too, just the day before, riding too fast downhill. Mother was crouched before me, peering up frowning into my face. "But why haven't you told me, Josie, if you'd hurt yourself? You used to tell Mother everything."

If once you start you might not be able to stop. So, I warn you!

Mother said, "When you were a little girl, remember how Mother would kiss where you'd been hurt, and make it well?"

My eyes smarted with tears. But I did not cry. I said, biting at my thumbnail, "I was afraid— afraid you'd scold."

In the library. In the marsh. In the library at his father's desk you see him, head in his hands. His narrow shoulders hunched, a pulse beating in his throat. He has removed his glasses, let them fall onto the desk. Still as death, Jared, Jr. While on the walls in shadow the mocking faces of Jesus Christ glare out at him. *Here we are! Here we are! Your savior!* In the marsh you see him, the oily-black length of him, moving slowly, sinuously; then coiling luxuriantly to sleep in the sun. His head, spade-shaped, of a terrifying ugliness, yet regal, imperturbable. And the golden-glowing eyes. You want to turn and run in panic but of course you can't, he won't release you. He has you now, he won't release you. The sun beats harder and harder in an accelerated rhythm on your head, against your eyelids. The marsh is filled with tittering, shrieking, grunting sounds—insects, birds, frogs, so many!—until at last the black snake rouses itself from its slumber to glide away, into the marsh. And not a backward glance.

Still as death, for hours. Icy-cold gone from my body. But then I return again. I'm never not watching you.

In the ruins of the old Presbyterian church. In the dry-crackling September heat, in the crumbling bricks, broken mortar, thistly weeds. Hidden from Trinity Street by a dense screen of vegetation, gorgeous flaming sumac. And here too the harsh startled cries of birds—blackbirds, starlings already flocking for migration. "Souls of the damned," Jared says, "always squawking." Whistling, leading you into the ruins following a narrow path up from the sidewalk; if observed by any neighbor it might appear that Jared Burkhardt, Jr. is going for an afternoon stroll, a meditative break from theology, with his young cousin Josie. Out of sight of the street Jared grips both your hands, your puny hands, in his. *He has you now: no escape.* It's a

Thursday afternoon, a school day. You left at your usual time but looped back slyly to hide in the marsh until Jared whistled for you. Marked *absent* at school in the ugly buff-brick factory-style building where your printed name is a joke: *Josephine Carolyn S———*. Jared wears his perfectly starched and ironed white long-sleeved shirt, opened at the throat. His hair has grown shaggy, glinting with metallic streaks. With his usual fastidiousness he removes his rimless round glasses, slides them into his shirt pocket; wipes his face with a white cotton handkerchief—one, in fact, monogrammed JBJ, you ironed yourself. Murmuring, "You're my prisoner, girl. Don't fight me!" Pushes you to the ground and straddles you. "Don't fight! You little bitch. You know better." You know that Jared hopes you will struggle so that he can overpower you, sharp-boned knee triumphant against your ribcage, long fingers closed teasingly around your neck. Precarious balance between *what Jared wants* and *what Jared does not want*. You are in terror of confusing the two, of provoking his genuine wrath. Too weak, too much in love to even pretend to struggle. For has Jared not disciplined you, *girl, wounded* you as he calls it?—how many times in the marsh and in the ruins of the old bridge. And now with strips of cheesecloth stolen from his grandmother's kitchen several times twisted for strength he binds your wrists and ankles. The soft cloth will leave no ugly bruises or incriminating marks, Jared thinks of such details, he is never not-thinking. Even in his sinewy snake-form never is he not-thinking. Never can you escape. Now hunched over you, his face flushed, the sunken eyes lit with excitement. Gaunt cheeks screwed up in exquisite revulsion. Behind his jerking-twitching head there is a cracked sky, storm-heavy clouds gathering, the heat will be broken by rain, flashes of incandescent lightning. Jared murmurs, mutters. His breath sharp, accelerating, peaking. "Just try! Try to fight . . . *me*. Filthy little—filthy, filth—*girl*." There's a wad of cheesecloth shoved into your mouth, you begin to choke, gag. Can't help it but you struggle, squirm, try to kick with your bound ankles. You're in terror, animal terror, beads of sweat breaking out like flame on your body. For hasn't Jared shown you in his bedroom in the secret locked drawers of his bureau certain magazines containing certain photographs . . . of girls your age, and younger; naked, cringing, terrified girls; a metaphysical astonishment in their brimming eyes; and bearing too their mysterious and hieroglyphic *wounds*. For all have been marked, all have been punished. "If you disobey your master," Jared has said.

Always faceless in the pulp-photos, these masters. Though parts of their bodies are suggested. Like God the Father hovering detached and observant at the margins of existence.

Did not do. Within my power. It's a later time, in fact bits of sleet are blown against the rattling window. Unless it's an earlier time? The grandfather clock in the downstairs parlor chimes an unknown hour. Ticklish nails, nipping teeth, run lightly over your body. Or not so lightly. Mother is away for a weekend in Port Oriskany and your great-aunt Esther Allan is at the medical center in Yewville for tests: She suffers from shortness of breath, wavering vision, a roaring "like Niagara" in her ears. Or is she simply an angry frightened ignorant old woman incapable of looking either forward or back. Jared, Jr. ever the attentive grandson drove his grandmother to the clinic and left her and now on his skinny haunches scrambling backward, skittering against the hardwood floor of his bedroom. His left eyelid droops lower than his right. Is that a glisten of blood on his mouth? It is over—it to which you have given no name—yet Jared is not triumphant, relieved; seems agitated and confused. Untying your wrists and ankles, his hands badly shaking.

"This . . . was an experiment! I tested myself, I stopped in time. You can see . . . I stopped in time! The challenge of life . . . " he tries to bring his breathing under control, he's sweating prodigiously and wiping his face on his sleeve, " . . . is to improvise, but to know when to stop, and I know. I did not do what it is within my power to do. *I did not do what it is within my power to do.*"

Helpless, spitting the gag from your mouth, you raise yourself onto your elbows and begin to vomit.

Love. Love. Love Jared, don't hurt me.

The Meaning of "Mother." This was another time long ago in a city of no name. Where one day (you were a little girl, you could not have been expected to comprehend) briskly whistling to herself, cheeks splotched with righteous indignation, your mother snatched an article of clothing out of a closet (it might have been the pretty floral-print robe your father had given her) and shook it hard as if shaking wrinkles from it, or sand. You'd followed her into the bedroom and there she stood waiting for you. "What is the meaning of 'Mother'? We all know that 'Mother' is warm, loving, forgiving, and not terribly bright. So let's put 'Mother' here." She laid the article of clothing onto the bed, positioned the upper part of it against the pillow with a certain mordant tenderness.

A long time later you were still crying, screaming in terror if any of them touched you.

The troublemaker. At Ransomville Junior High School where I am the youngest in my class, in seventh grade. Thin-armed, dark-eyed, furtive. Known for my dreaminess and my grades of A though there are at least two teachers who hate me. I am a mysterious new girl in a school of boys and girls who've known one another all their lives. With a peculiar nervous mannerism of grinning when I'm startled, or frightened. And an easily upset stomach — "gas pains." If once you start. I warn you. But I never cry even when, in gym class, certain of the bigger girls gang up against me and send me flying to the floor.

Mostly I stare out the window bored by my teachers. Though the winter clouds are bulbous and oozing (I don't want to look, I can't help looking) slime. One of my teachers, angry hurt eyes like I'm to blame for her ugly frog-face, is forever calling on me, quizzing me. "Why are you looking out the window, 'Josephine'?—what is of such fascination to you outside the window?" The name "Josephine" on her curled lips is rightly ridiculous, no wonder the class erupts with gales of imbecile laughter. My revenge is to be perfect. My revenge is to dig my nails into my flesh, the soft inner arm, until I draw blood. These too are *wounds* of a kind. Oddly, Jared never notices.

In the marsh. In the library. Beneath the collapsed bridge. In Jared's bedroom, the door safely locked.

It's a fact of life, inhabiting two places simultaneously. As one fades out like a weak radio station the other grows stronger, vivid as the most compelling dream.

One day I decide, at school, to take control of the laughing. To be *funny on purpose.* Maybe I'll be *popular,* then, too—don't all seventh-grade girls want to be *popular?*

Squirming like a demented eel at my desk, twining my hair in my fingers, peeking over my shoulders at the boys catching their eyes as if I'm one of them. *Look, look at me! Laugh at me!* There can't be anything serious or sad or shameful about Josephine S———, the class clown, can there? My brilliantly sarcastic quips evoke gasps even when the teacher doesn't quite hear. "What was that, Josephine?" "Oh, um—" smirking behind my hand, "nothing." Sent by a teacher to the blackboard to demonstrate a problem in long division that leaves most of the class stumped, I ply the chalk skillfully as any adult, yet have time to coyly roll my eyes behind the teacher's back even as I'm being praised; what pleasure in stirring titters, giggles! What curious power! Old Frogface who hated my guts lost control and shook me once at my desk, another time after class spoke to me alone with as much wonderment as anger, "It's virtually unknown, an A-student, an obviously intelligent girl, a *troublemaker!*" I was amazed, embarrassed. I stammered, "It is? I mean—I *am?*"

The black snake. Mother was driving on the River Road, the wind whipping swaths of snow up into the headlights and across the windshield and Mother's wine-sweetened breath and perfume making my temples ache and I shaped *Jared,*

Jared in the way of a prayer so yearning! so lonely! for it had been days since he had so much as glanced at me, glancing coolly passing me silently in the *Reverend's house* and almost immediately there was, on the road rushing toward us, a black snake!—strangely stretched out, covering the width of the road which must have been fifteen feet!—and I screamed, "No! Don't hit it! No! *Stop!*" as Mother drove her car over the snake, I felt the terrible *thud* as the car's wheels passed over it and screamed and screamed and struck at Mother with my fists, "The snake! You killed him! No—!" Mother was astonished, braking the car to a stop shuddering on the shoulder of the road as the wind blew rocking the car like our racing heartbeats and she said, "Are you crazy? That wasn't a snake, that was a strip of tar across the road! Did you want me to crash the car, did you want to cause an accident? What's wrong with you, Josie? *You hit your mother.*" In a cold fury now seeing how I cringed in shame and mortification, Mother slapped me on the side of my face, turned her hand to slap a second time so her new square-cut sapphire ring cut into my left cheek and the blood sprang out pent-up hot like a long-inheld breath and Mother cursed, "Damn you! Look at you! And your new jacket—" and fumbled for a tissue to wipe at my face, and another, and another, and we sat huddled together pressing the wad of tissues against my bleeding cheek and Mother said half-sobbing, "Oh Christ! I'm sorry," and I mumbled in shame, "It's all right."

Children of Noah. It was one of the books from the Reverend's library, Jared, Jr. invited me into the library to see it, I was shy opening it wondering what was expected of me? to make some sort of intelligent commentary on a work of Biblical history? but why would Jared, Jr. care for any thoughts of *mine?*—as he stood by the desk by lamplight his attention seemingly divided between a notebook in which he was writing, and me, as awkwardly with a quizzical-hopeful smile I leafed through the book, it was old and its pages brittle and dog-eared and even the print of its pages seemed fussy and old-fashioned, and the titles of its chapters "The Genealogy of the Patriarchs," "The Construction of the Ark," "God's Covenant with Noah," and I turned a page and saw a photograph of a young girl slipped into the book, it *was myself*, lying twisted on her back and her wrists and ankles bound and her naked body covered in cobwebbed markings of cuts, bruises, burns—her eyes thinly shut, her lips drawn back from her teeth in a frozen grimace of pain and incredulity, myself though younger, even skinnier than me, more piteous, her pale hair growing in thin tufts like a sickly chicken, I saw, I stared, my fingers weakened and the book fell and I fumbled to retrieve it as Jared said, "What is it you're seeing, girl? Something you shouldn't be seeing?" watching me closely, his lips pursed, "Something forbidden? Eh, girl? Is it?" The intonation of his words seemed to me those of an older man, not his own.

A sound behind me and with quicksilver poise Jared glanced over my shoulder at Aunt Esther!—standing in the doorway twisting her hands in her apron, I could not face her, dared not face her, there came a roaring in my ears and my vision had gone and Jared was telling his grandmother in his polite boyish voice that he'd been showing me some theology classics at my request but I was finding them hard to read.

Aunt Esther said primly, "I shouldn't wonder. Books like that are for grown-up people, men with a calling to God, not junior high school girls."

Stared and stared at such evidence Jared set before me. For I saw these photographs as proof not of evil but of adult knowledge as the encyclopedias in the public library were filled with knowledge I did not and could not know. These photographs of bound and tortured and possibly dying or dead children as proof of a forbidden wisdom not taught to us nor even hinted to us at school. For the *Covenant* would not be with children, would it?

The black hawk. And in the form of a black hawk too Jared slipped from his body leaving his body empty, cold, glassy-eyed; the beautiful black-feathered wide-winged sharp-beaked hawk climbed the sky in lazy-looking spirals then as you held your breath dropped swiftly to dive into the snowy marsh to seize its prey which were smaller birds, blue jays, chickadees, sparrows defenseless against its superior size and strength and the cunning of its attack and no evidence remained atop the snow except scattered bloody feathers, marks of flailing wings, for the black hawk lifted its prey in its talons and flew away to devour it and these winter days (as Jared pointed out through a rear attic window) the hawk perched on the very roof of the house, or on the roof of the old garage, though mostly on the uppermost limbs of certain trees along the river as

Jared sent me with his mind, guided me along the path in the direction of town *You'll have to be punished! unless you punish another in your place!* so in my boots, jeans, fleece-lined jacket and wool cap pulled low over my forehead looking as much a boy as a girl and of no identity whatsoever I made my way in stealth on certain *missions of retribution.* Jared was revulsed by poor-white trash as he and his grandmother called the inhabitants of the houses of poorer neighborhoods, downtown in Ransomville you would see groups of the loud-laughing hulking sexually mature boys and girls of high school age, boys with blemished skins and the beginnings of beards and hoarse, crack-ing, derisive voices, the girls who were female before they were women, with powerful thigh muscles, budding breasts straining against the fabric of their bright vulgar cheerful clothes, how Jared, Jr. shrank from them! the contempla-tion of them, and their careless prowling eyes! *cattle!* he called them *breeders!* And into their world I would descend guided by the slow-circling hawk in the sky, the hawk's icy-unwavering eye, once on a Sunday near dusk I was drawn to the shouts and cries of skaters on the river, children sledding on a hill whose hard-packed snow was trailed with sled marks like the raking of myriad

nails in silk. *If the ice on the river would crack! if the vermin would drown! if the plagues of Sodom and Gomorrah might sweep upon these!* I passed among the teenagers and children silent and watchful and if any knew me, called my name, I seemed not to hear, my eyes shrank away, the spirit of Jared filled me deep as breath. A *mission of retribution* might be: setting a small fire in a garage, a shed, the rear of a shabby ramshackle house. Shattering a window with a rock. Noting, at dusk, where windows were dark, to dare to enter by a rear, unlocked door (for it was rare for doors to be locked in Ransomville, especially during the day) guided by Jared's thoughts *Do. Go. As I say.* Seeking an *offering,* cheap-framed photograph of a smiling married couple, a radiantly happy young mother holding a baby in her arms, a proud-smiling teenager in a high school cap and gown, an old tarnished heart-shaped locket, a child's panda or doll, any *offering* that was evidence of human contamination as Jared called it, secular love, any *offering* that would be missed. And these items to be stolen and smuggled out inside my jacket as invisibly I slipped away with amazing composure, fearlessness *not my own but his* for I knew that no one could touch me nor even see me so long as the black hawk prevailed.

And these items brought to Jared where he waited sometimes in the marsh, or beneath the ruins of the old bridge, or in the ruins of the old Presbyterian church above Trinity Street where with tremulous gloved hands, squatting, muttering to himself, angry-seeming though smiling, his breath steaming about him in spurts, he would prepare the *sacrifice*, which was a small fire safely ringed about by bricks, hunks of concrete, icy-crusted snow. How dreamy we were, shutting our eyes in the flames' bright heat!

Always afterward Jared was in high spirits. Love for me shone in his eyes, unmistakable. For after all, Jared had only me to do his bidding; only me, of all the world, to entrust with his mission. Seeing how I gazed upon him in adoration he laughed, drew his thumbs in twin caressing gestures across my cheeks as if to stretch the skin — "A little less filth in the world, eh, girl? 'Cousin Josie'? Not much, but it's a start."

The wild. In late January Mother disappeared from Ransomville for twelve days with no explanation except there were "crucial matters to be sorted through" leaving only a scribbled note for me to discover when I came home from school; to Aunt Esther, she'd said nothing at all. The old woman was incensed, appalled; talked of little else in the days Mother was away; saying repeatedly, to me, "What kind of a woman would do such a thing! What kind of a mother! Not to think of her own daughter, or her own relatives!—just to go run away God knows where." Silent then regarding me with eyes that seemed as much gloating as sympathetic. And wondering too of course whether I had any idea where my mother had gone. "I pity Delia, I do. She may be a 'glamorous' woman but that doesn't last forever, it's the *immortal soul* that lasts forever. Once you cross a certain line, into the wild, anything is possible."

The crucifixion. Feel yourself drawn! As in a dream along the river path trampled by numberless feet, a sharply cold day in February, a jellied-pale sky against which the steep-pitched roofs of houses look unreal as drawings in a children's book of fairy tales. *Go. Do. As I say* Jared has commanded. *A finger. A hand. A heart.*

This time, a living prey.

Blood sacrifice, it's time. Did not Abraham obey God?—Jared has recited to you the thrilling words of Genesis. Not for you to judge.

Are you frightened?—*fear is good, fear is normal.*

Are you in terror of the black hawk overhead, its terrible talons, beak?—*fear will save your life.*

Walking with a girl you've befriended on the hill, sweet child, five years old perhaps, sadly watching the older children sledding and they've ignored her such a pretty little girl though her nose is running so you wipe it with a tissue, somehow her mittened hand is in your hand, her name is Bobbie, she's chattering excitedly and *you have her: no escape* like any big sister walking a little sister home listening to her chatter along the river and approaching the rear of the ramshackle woodframe house where the horses, mule, goats, and pigs are penned which is Bobbie's house she says tugging at your hand but you tell her you're taking her to your house for just a little visit, wouldn't she like to come and visit your house that's only a block or two away, there's hot chocolate, there's gingerbread cookies, there's ice cream, a baby-sized doll for her to play with, so she says OK, hardly an instant's hesitation. High above, the black hawk sways in the wind, the yellow-glaring eye of the hawk calm, all-seeing, rapt upon its prey. For Jared says *The fact of the crucifixion is the center of our faith but it doesn't matter who is crucified, only that one innocent and without sin is crucified.* Now leading little Bobbie uphill in the direction of Trinity Street, big sister and little sister giggling together, breaths steaming. In one of Jared's secret photographs you've seen Bobbie already, you'd recognized her, so it's an accomplished fact, it's fate. Already it has happened—it to which you've given no name—so you are powerless to prevent it, and blameless. As, by night, in your bed on the second floor of the *Reverend's house* you feel the deep sucking pit of time in the very foundation of the house, into which you will be drawn one day unnamed, naked, even your bones devoured clean, and scattered. Not your mother's *Josie*, or *baby*; not Jared's *girl*.

(Mother!—whom you've vowed never to call "Mother" again. Since her return from the mysterious absence—to Coral Gables, Florida, where she'd been taken by a new man friend to spend some "private, very special time together.")

The child Bobbie is asking what is your name, and her nose is running again so you squat before her to wipe it, you see her eyes blinking at you in utter trust and something turns in your heart though the black hawk is high overhead *Go. Do. As I say.* And in that instant you change your mind and seizing Bobbie's hand you lead her back in the direction of her home, her mother is calling her you say, can't she hear her mother calling her?—and at the edge of the animals' pen you release her and she runs toward the back door of the house without so much as a backward glance nor will she remember you even a few minutes later. Is the hawk watching? astonished, furious? You don't look up, you run away eyes downcast, heart beating in terror of being seized by razor-sharp ripping talons, the horror of the hawk's beak stabbing at your eyes as Jared has warned, you come to a ravine where old mattresses, broken furniture, household trash have been dumped, discovering as if *this too is fate: sent by God as Abraham was sent the ram* a rubber doll, filthy, naked, headless; a little-girl doll; you shake snow from it, carry it inside your jacket to the *Reverend's house* where later that afternoon Jared will discover it on his father's desk.

Sick. Screaming at you, spitting at you, cursing— "Filthy little bitch, didn't obey me. Didn't do as I said. *Betrayed me!*" He has torn the rubber doll apart, sobbing in fury, frustration, he's thrown the pieces onto the floor now gripping you by the nape of your neck, forcing you to your knees where you're mute, unresisting. *Jared forgive me*

you can't say *Jared I love you*. But the touch of you burns his fingers, he recoils in disgust. Shoves you from him, kicks you to the floor as if the mere sight of you, the smell of you, is revolting to him. He paces about his room bringing his fists together, hair disheveled, shirt torn open at the throat, "Just makes me sick! All of it! All of you! Sick! *Sick!*" As if the word, the hissing furious sound *sick! sick! sick* is mesmerizing to him.

Then abruptly, as it has happened in the past, it's over: Jared wipes his face, adjusts his clothing, backs off. Almost, at such a moment, he looks repentant; almost ethereal, like the most radiant of the several depictions of Jesus Christ on the wall of the library. In a low, bemused voice saying, "It was only an experiment, 'Josie.' It wasn't real. None of it was real. It never has been real. It was only to test you. Now, get out."

How have I failed him? — poor Aunt Esther, for weeks complaining bitterly and helplessly to your mother about Jared, Jr.'s increasingly erratic behavior. Suddenly it has happened, with no apparent provocation, that Jared has been brooding, short-tempered and excitable; locks his doors and refuses to allow her, or the cleaning woman, to enter his part of the house — even to change his towels and bedclothes. "And you know how clean, how spotlessly clean, Jared likes to keep himself!" Most upsetting, Jared refuses to eat virtually all of the meals she so carefully prepares for him; has several times, in her presence, thrown dishes onto the floor and cursed her as a "damned old harpy" and a "meddling old fool." Dabbing at her eyes, piteous in her dismay, the elderly woman confides in her niece Delia who is astonished by the sudden revelations of Burkhardt family secrets, like coins carelessly spilled out onto the carpet—that Jared, Sr. also suffered from "mental seizures" that came upon him out of the blue and caused "tragic sorrow" among his loved ones; that Jared, Sr. might have been responsible for the fire that destroyed his church—"Though not a shred of evidence was ever found against him"; that Jared, Jr., as young as eight years, began to exhibit too similar signs of "religious excitement" and "mental agitation"—though of course, as Aunt Esther hastened to say, Jared was always a very good boy, a very sweet and obedient boy, a saintly boy, in every way *a boy blessed by God*. It is revealed, too, that Jared, Jr. has had several episodes of what his Rochester physicians called "nervous exhaustion," which forced him to interrupt his seminary education intermittently for years. "And now it looks as if Jared might not be able to return to the seminary this spring, as he's been planning," Aunt Esther tells Mother. "Oh Delia, how have I failed the boy? What have I done wrong?"

"I assume you've prayed for him, Aunt Esther?"

"Prayed for him?—of course. Every hour of every day since this terrible thing began!"

"Then Jared's fate is in the hands of God," Mother says somberly, by this time bored with the elderly woman's nonsense, and backing discreetly from the room. "I would not contest His great plan for all of us, Aunt Esther, if I were you."

Gone. Through March and into April it seemed that my mother was involved with a mysterious man friend whose name I never learned but her plans changed, or were changed, as in a violent windstorm, daily or even hourly. What roaring winds, what abrupt alterations of temperature, as the earth veered to spring! And one evening Mother returned early, distraught, to the *Reverend's house* and her breath smelled of whiskey, and her skin was dead-white, and for a long moment she stared at me where I lay curled up on her bed sucking at my fingers waiting for her, stared as if she didn't recognize me; then uttering a little cry she came to me and gathered me in her arms; hid her heated damp face in my neck, shivering, hugging me as she had not hugged me in years. "Oh, Josie, I've neglected you, haven't I? You're growing up, you're no longer a child, soon you'll be a woman and I'm to blame for not seeing. But I've been so unhappy, I've been so *undefined*. Every man I've ever wanted, when I have him I cease to want him—it's a curse. And God Himself has broken my heart with His false promises. It used to be, God used men and women for His purposes, and though some of these were, well, jokes, tricks—at least, He used us. Now, He has lost interest. You can pray and pray and it's like dropping a rock into the Grand Canyon. Before the rock hits bottom, you're gone."

You would not call it love you would call it by another name.

Forcing the lock to your cousin Jared's door and tiptoeing into his bedroom (the dimensions of which look smaller than you recall, your memory distended by terror) and there forcing, with a stilettolike letter opener from the desk in the library, the lock to the forbidden bureau drawer, and you discover—*the drawer is empty*.

You grope inside, but there's nothing. Jared has destroyed it all.

The lurid pulp-paper magazines, the hideous photographs of bound, tortured, naked female children, your own twin sister among them, and the child Bobbie: gone!

Helplessly you weep, in infinite relief.

Fear is good, normal. Fear will save your life.

You're in a state of exaltation, frightened though in truth you are not in much danger of being discovered: Aunt Esther has been confined to her room following a stroke in late March, overseen by round-the-clock registered nurses; Jared, Jr. recovered from his "nervous exhaustion" and returned to the seminary in Rochester in time for the spring quarter; Delia S——— is away, on a visit as she'd vaguely explained, with an old, dear friend, in another part of the state.

After the headless rubber doll, after your betrayal of him as he called it—Jared has never spoken to you again. Nor ever will.

How peaceful now, how lonely the *Reverend's house.* That deep pit of fathomless time yawning beneath it, you have not the courage to contemplate.

And so, why attempt it? Instead, you stand at one of Jared's windows overlooking a newly budded chestnut tree in the front lawn; you struggle to lift the window, push it halfway up, inhaling with a shock of pleasure the cool, fresh air. Late April, yet it's the first real day of spring. A blue-windy, brilliant day, eagerly you open your heart to the vast sky tracked by long diaphanous clouds stretching for what appear to be hundreds of miles, you hear birds, songbirds, newly returned from south after the long winter, their exquisite sweet spring cries.

About the Author

JOYCE CAROL OATES is the author of numerous works of fiction, poetry, criticism, and drama. Among her most recent books are *Zombie*, *What I Lived For*, *The Perfectionist and Other Plays*, and *George Bellows: American Artist*. A past recipient of the National Book Award and a member of the American Academy and Institute of Arts and Letters, she is the Roger S. Berlind Distinguished Professor in the Humanities at Princeton University.

* * *

About the Illustrator

BARRY MOSER has illustrated and designed nearly 200 titles, including the Arion Press *Moby-Dick* and the University of California Press *The Divine Comedy of Dante*. His edition of Lewis Carroll's *Alice's Adventures in Wonderland*, won the National Book Award for design and illustration in 1983. Mr. Moser lives in western Massachusetts.